A
ANTICS!
Z

ANTICS!

An Alphabetical **Ant**hology

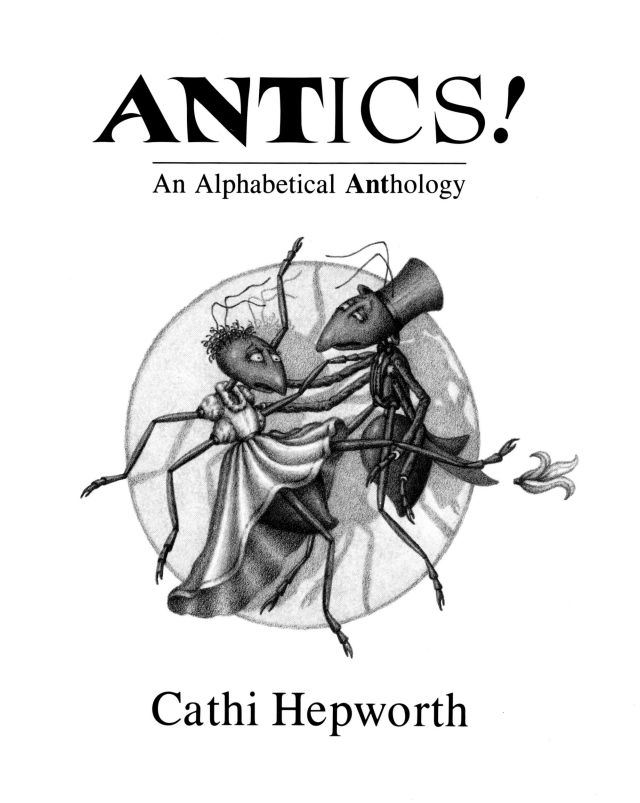

Cathi Hepworth

G. P. PUTNAM'S SONS · NEW YORK

A

G. P. Putnam's Sons, a division of The Putnam & Grosset Book Group,
200 Madison Avenue, New York, NY 10016.
Published simultaneously in Canada
Printed in Hong Kong by South China Printing Co. (1988) Ltd.

Library of Congress Cataloging-in-Publication Data
Hepworth, Catherine.
Antics! : an alphabet of ants / by Cathi Hepworth.
p. cm.
Summary: Alphabetical entries from A to Z all have an "ant" somewhere
in the word: There's E for Enchanter, P for Pantaloons, S for Santa
Claus, and Y for Your Ant Yetta.
1. English language—Alphabet—Juvenile literature.
[1. Alphabet.] I. Title.
PE1155.H47   1992   91-2672 CIP AC
421'.1—dc20
ISBN 0-399-21862-9

1   3   5   7   9   10   8   6   4   2
First Impression

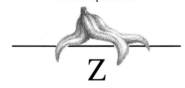

Z

For Brad,
and for Mom, Dad, Dave,
John, Jenni, Becki, and Ami…
"the Neandersons"

Antique

Brilliant

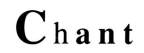

Chant

Deviant

Enchanter

Flamboyant

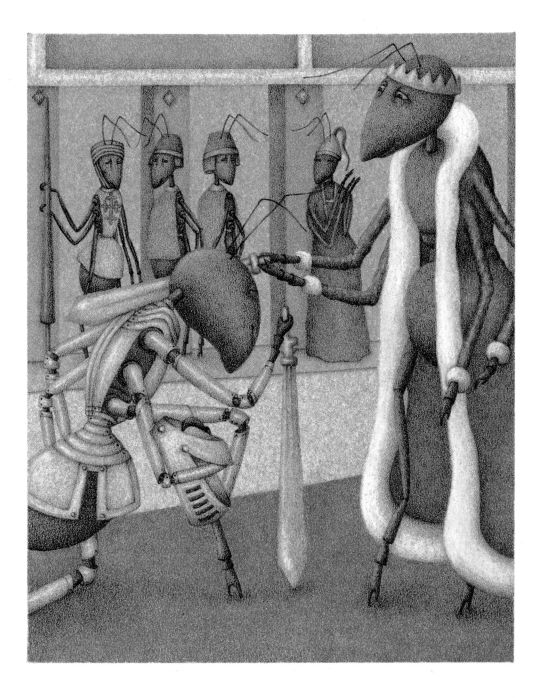

Gallant

Hesit**ant**

Immigrants

Jubil**ant**

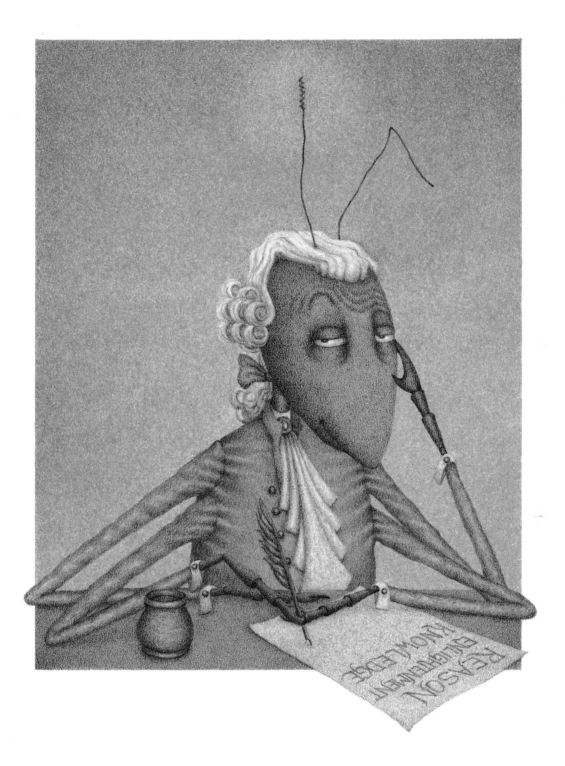

K a n t

Lieutenant

Mutant

Nonchalant

Observant

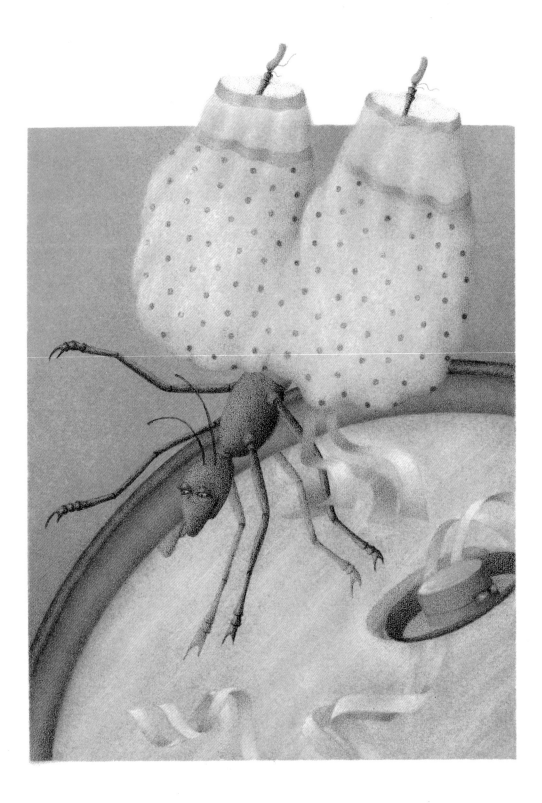

Pantaloons

Quarantine

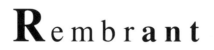

Rembra**n**t

Santa Claus

Tantrum

Unpleas**ant**

Vigilantes

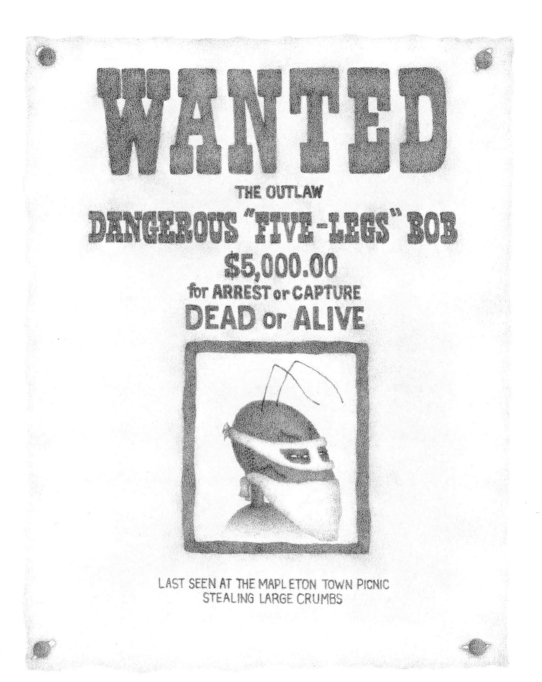

Wanted

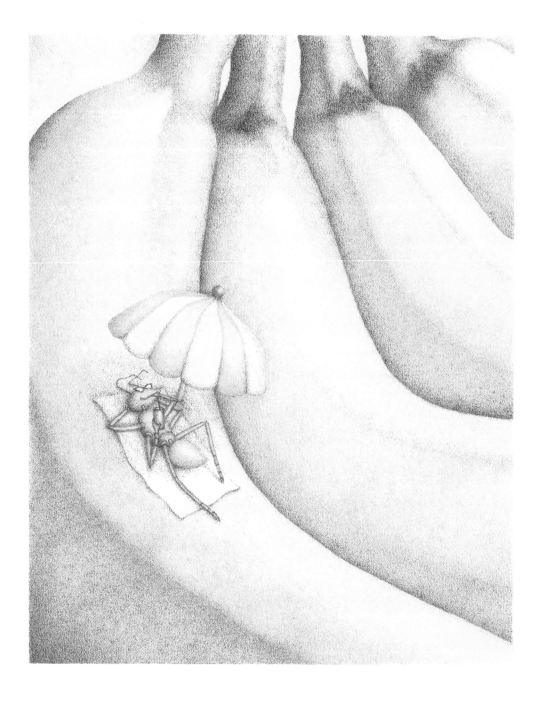

Xanthophile

Your **A**nt Yetta

Antzzzzzz